HOLDING

STONES

HOLDING

STONES

ROBERTA DEWA

Published by
Pewter Rose Press
17 Mellors Rd,
West Bridgford
Nottingham, NG2 6EY
United Kingdom
www.pewter-rose-press.com

First published in Great Britain 2009

ISBN 978-0-9560053-1-1

British Library Cataloguing in Publication Data
A catalogue record for this book is available from the British Library

Cover design by www.thedesigndepot.co.uk

Printed and bound in Great Britain by the MPG Books Group

Pewter Rose Press
www.pewter-rose-press.com

CONTENTS

ACKNOWLEDGEMENTS

The stories in this collection were written over a fairly extended period, and I want to express my gratitude to Sheelagh Gallagher, in whose writing group many of them first saw the light of day, and whose wise comments helped me along the way. I would also like to thank the editors of the publications in which some of the stories first appeared. *Sleeping Beauty* was published in *3D: New Fiction and Poetry*, 2006. *Victoria* was published online at pulp.net, December 2005. *Reservoir, Lazarus,* and *Holding Stones* were published in *Staple* (Issues 61: Winter 2004, 65: Summer 2006, and 67: Winter 2007). I should also like to thank particularly Anne and Nick McDonnell of Pewter Rose Press for their help and interest, and for the opportunity to see *Holding Stones* in print for the first time as a collection. Finally, special thanks to my husband Peter for that most difficult of all supportive roles – that of living with a writer.

FOREWORD

In life, I have often noticed how the past does not stay in its place. So it is for many of the characters in these stories, who are haunted or visited by the past: old lovers return, dead lovers speak from the grave; or the characters are lost or stranded in the present, drawing the past like a blanket around themselves, dwelling in a twilit region that estranges them both from the outside world, and from one another. Relationships between men and women seem to offer closeness, but reveal estrangement too: as do the relationships of Bleaklow, of Repossession, of Sleeping Beauty. But, though some of the characters seek escape, they are not passive victims of their own histories. I notice how often it is the women who hold on, who try to wrest meaning from persistent memory: the grieving woman who must repeatedly climb a mountain; the woman who guards her wilderness of garden against the destructiveness of her neighbours; the woman who strains to hear the voices of a drowned village.

And I notice especially two images I have used to express the presence of the past. In Victoria, the bereaved protagonist feels the comfort of her lover's cold hands in her pocket; in Holding

Stones, the title story, Susan signifies acceptance of the past as a stone held in the hand. Both are images of loss, but they are also images of a companion that never leaves us. Although we are often rebuked for living in the past, memory is a mechanism for understanding, a way of knowing who it is we are; it reminds us of the selves we once were, and that, for better or worse, we are still.

I believe that stories reach a very deep part of us. Given that as human beings we are all alone, all made strangers in some sense to one another, stories can still make a kind of connection with our singularity. They do not always comfort the stranger within us; but always they offer company, a way to be less alone.

Roberta Dewa

www.robertadewa.co.uk

HOLDING STONES

In the cafe behind the beach there is a map showing where the new road will go. The map is homemade, roughly framed and hung on the wall, an aerial view of the coastline with the hills poster-painted in bright green, and a royal blue sea edging up to meet them. The road is a thick line of red paint pushing its way between green and blue, past the headland and running the length of the seafront. About halfway along the line, the words THIS CAFE are written in bold black capitals beside a thick black arrow. Both words and arrow seem to be adrift, floating out to sea, pointing back towards the seashore, to an invisible spot along the beach.

Underneath the map, one of the cafe tables has been pushed back against the wall. On top of the table is an unused Accounts Book, a pencil on a string lying in the centre of its open pages. A note below the book asks patrons to sign the petition before they leave.

The door at the back of the cafe stands open, and the sound of trickling water comes from the sunny tea-garden beyond. The fountain too is homemade, like everything else in the cafe, constructed from thin tubes of metal bent and painted green to look like the stems of a plant, the central tube topped by a red plastic windmill that looks vaguely like a sunflower. Somebody's child has trotted across the grass and deposited two pennies in the miniature pillarbox beside the fountain; the child stands watching as the green tubes gush water and the red sunflower turns.

The fountain runs for two minutes, then stops.

Susan and her mother are making their way carefully from the promenade down to the sand. It's a slow business, teetering across the piles of round pebbles swept up by the sea and left in hard grey mounds below the promenade. Her mother's white feet are in sensible brown buckled sandals and her skin never tans. Susan is wearing her first pair of navy Scholls, her legs Darjeeling colour, thumping her thick wooden soles down the pebbles to the sand, ready to dash out onto it the minute the ebb tide lets it go.

Her mother comes down after her. They take their sandals off and the first wavy line of sand sinks slightly under their toes. The sea backs slowly away from them, letting the wind dry out the beach, loosening up the sand into grains of beige mist that sting their ankles. Susan watches the waves running simultaneously forward and backward in that curious way they do when the tide is going out. She doesn't ask if they can swim yet. Instead she rolls up the bottoms of her Bri-nylon slacks, ready for paddling.

"Wait till late afternoon," says her mother, looking at the waves. "When the tide turns."

"Or the moon will suck you out to sea," says Susan, hopping about in the chilly shallows.

Her mother finds a good firm stretch of sand and puts the Gladstone bag down. This bag holds a rug, a pale green Thermos, sandwiches and a good supply of towels. The rug flaps in the wind as she shakes it out, hovers briefly in the air and then settles on the warm sand. Susan leaves her putting out the cups and follows the waves as they recede, waiting for them to start lapping on the edge of the first sandbank, the one where the shells collect. While she paddles, once the water's washed up to her calves, she looks back.

Her mother is sitting on the rug, hands around drawn-up knees, facing out to sea as if she's looking at her daughter, though it's hard to be sure, because her eyes are hidden behind her thick dark prescription sunglasses.

Susan's mother has weak eyes, like her father before her. Like her father before her she says little, never complains of heat, of cold, of pain. At the hospital where he died they told Susan and her mother that he just faded quietly away.

The cafe owner is assembling a Knickerbocker Glory. He assembles it on top of the counter, in full view of the customers. Hundreds and thousands rain down onto a swirl of whipped cream, a worm of chocolate sauce squeezes from a brown plastic bottle over a scoop of vanilla ice cream. Further down, a scoop of strawberry, tinned raspberries, another scoop of vanilla and an inch of dark sweet purple blackcurrant sauce to fill up the thick glass base.

"Are you going on the beach?" he says to the little girl in his high, falsetto voice, inserting the long spoon very carefully into the mixture.

She nods her head.

"Mind you don't go swimming until you've digested."

A group of older children drinking milkshakes at a table near the door laugh when they hear the cafe owner's voice. They nudge each other and snigger at his painted-on brown eyebrows and his chestnut-coloured wig. This child does not laugh but watches with a solemnity, a seriousness, as the glass fills, the colours run one into the other, the white frozen globe sinks and melts down into the purple syrup. When the process is complete, she holds up her arm and rests her hand against the counter, the gunmetal shine of two half-crowns between her fingers.

"That's the right money, thank you," he says, his voice rising with the light end of the word, lowering the heavy glass towards the child. "Be careful with that now."

He receives the coins and turns them over in his hand, feeling the weight of them, the rib of the hard milled edge. Holds one of them up, edge towards the child.

"The half crown's got a rough edge, do you see, not a smooth one. That's so a blind man can tell them from pennies."

She nods, her hands linked with one another around the cold glass base.

"Do you know what D-day is?" he says to her.

She nods again, this time more slowly, afraid of disturbing the contents of the glass.

"It was in the war. Mummy told me."

"Your mother is quite right," he says, "But there's another one, coming soon. Not a war, a big change. One that means this money won't be money any more."

Her eyes widen. The heavy glass shakes slightly in her hands.

"Never mind," he says. "Never mind. You enjoy your ice cream now."

The little girl walks slowly to the table with her burden. The cafe owner pushes the till drawer shut. Then he drops the half-crowns carefully, one at a time, into the pocket of his sand-brown overall.

The moon is still pulling the sea away. Susan follows it, over the deep soft sandbank, through the stranded pools and hard ridges and spiky caddis-worm casts, down to the low water mark. Close-to, the edge of the sea bubbles creamily with something, the water is mottled with dark specks of rubbish, thickened with seaweed, a soup of surface and depths. There are seagulls here, low-water seagulls that don't squall the way they do on the promenade but stay quiet, that seem half asleep, resting on the wind blowing over her head. The Irish Sea heaves with breakers that refuse to break. It too is asleep, dreaming grey salty dreams, its water heavy as mercury, peeling back from the seabed. In the foam of the last few receding waves the dead things appear, the long white skins of dogfish, the pale green limbs of crabs scattered by the gulls. Fingernail-pink butterfly shells lodged in the sand, the buried wing always shattered.

The sea pauses at the moment of low tide, tense, waiting for the swing of the moon.

When Susan looks round her mother is still there, tiny but alert, sitting up very straight as if keeping watch. Way above her head the clouds are piled into mounds of sky, a grey mist dropped over the hills, over the thin white line of beach huts, the promenade, the grey uneven line of pebbles. A sky filling and darkening with water, getting ready to fall.

Susan starts to retrace her steps. She feels the tide turn at her back, lapping slowly at her heels.

The cafe owner is cashing up. Dad has come down from the bungalow on the far side of the tea garden to help with the crockery, piling cups and saucers onto a tin tray, taking them through to the kitchen and coming back for more. Now and again he talks to the customers, tells them about when the first coast road was pushed through the headland in the thirties, about the noise and dynamite and the dust of the stones raining down on the beach.

When they make for the petition he shakes his head.

At ten past five he goes out of the cafe by the back door to make his way slowly across the lawn to the bungalow, to begin the task of getting tea ready. He moves silently in his brown slippers, dipping his head to pass the trellis draped with clematis that shades the outside tables, his white cotton jacket catching the sun as he moves out into the garden. Halfway across the lawn he stops and unlocks the pillarbox beside the fountain to empty out the takings. The mechanism that starts the fountain is finely set, tipped by the half an ounce that is the precise weight of two pennies. It will need adjusting when the old money goes.

When Dad has gone, the cafe owner walks over to the map. There are three new signatures on the petition since this morning: a family from Widnes, a Miss Broadbridge from Knutsford, an entry with no name in wavy child's writing:

I liked the painting.

He stands back and looks at his map. In this light he sees the open spaces filled with solid colour, the outlines hard and black as they never are in life, the hills flat slabs of green, the sea a frozen patch of blue. The road red, as real roads are on real maps. He closes the book, places the pencil neatly below it and moves backward until he is standing in the way of the sunlight, in the centre of his cafe; one hand at his side, one hand closed around the half-crowns in his pocket. Behind him, the round pools of purple metal tables, the crossed legs of chairs, the salty glisten of the sugar-bowls. He stands to attention, while the shafts of sunlight cut through him, carve the shape of his shadow on the blue glossed floor. The shadow moves, though so slowly he will never see it. Moves with the earth, till the sun gives way to the moon.

He turns round, looks through the open doorway. Dad has reached the four stone steps that lead from the garden up to the bungalow. He puts his hand out to the rail and his white summer jacket flashes like a flag, like the light on a windscreen. The old man is shrinking fast, retreating back into a tent of skin and bones, drawing the jacket like a sail around his memories, carrying them far away, out to sea.

The door opens, slowly closes on him. The garden falls into silence. The red sunflower gleams plastic in the evening sun.

"Didn't you bring anything back?"

Susan shakes her head. While she has been away her mother has made a small collection of pale pink shells, spread out to dry on the rug beside her. Susan brushes the sand from her calves and takes a clean towel from the bag to dry her feet. Her toes are dirty, the tidemark of the foam a crusty line traced around her ankles.

"I don't feel like swimming today. Can we swim tomorrow instead?"

Her mother nods and starts to gather up her shells, putting them into the empty sandwich bag, rolling the brown paper edges, putting the bag into her pocket. She stays quiet, tilting her sunglasses like a telescope, as the sun shifts its angle. While the tide creeps in they retreat to the stones and perch there, the rug folded beneath them, the Gladstone bag packed and tidy at their backs.

They stay till the last of the sand.

After the men with dynamite have been and gone, after the dust has settled, Susan comes back to the seaside town. She comes back, not once but year after year, parking her car on the strip of black tarmac that forms the new promenade, getting out to walk on the beach.

When she comes back the tide is always in. No matter what time of the day it is, no matter how she tries to second-guess the movement of the sea, the tide is always in, tiny waves sucking at the stones, the dull murk of the seabed creeping slowly onshore. Now, beyond the promenade, there is a high grey concrete wall that screens the new road from the beach. From behind the wall comes the long sharp scouring sound of invisible lorries on their way to Holyhead, their great blunt noses tracking west along the coast, smelling the ships that will take them to Ireland. They never stop except for repairs, for the changing of a tyre to replace black shreds of rubber strewn along the carriageway.

There is a single breach in the wall. A tunnel for pedestrians burrows underneath the road, a tunnel linking the new promenade with the old town, with the old cafe. There is a small estate of council houses gathered round a cul-de-sac on the plot of land where the cafe used to be. The cul-de-sac is named, Llys Sambrook, after the last cafe owner.

Susan does not use the tunnel. She stays on the promenade, stumbles down onto the pebbles, faces seaward.

On each visit, before she leaves, she shuts her eyes and bends down to the beach, placing her hands on the broken rocks and the broken shells, searching and feeling for the thing she is looking for. When she makes her way back to the car, she is holding stones, one in each hand, smooth rounded granite, grey and dense with the weight of the seabed in them. As she drives away she feels the slow dark roll of them in the echo chamber of the boot, while the road unwinds.

This story is dedicated to the memory of dear old Penmaenmawr.

The Peace Dividend

Today, life begins.

I mean of course a second life, since I have both reached the age of forty and am about to be married. Therefore it is right that I should date my existence — in the social language of maxim, which belongs to us all, and unlike us travels through time unscathed — from the present, in the present.

For all this I am indebted to Patrick. I am one who was born, as Conrad said, like a man who falls into a dream, and it has been Patrick's task not to wake me from that dream, but to explain it and thus enable me to place it in my mind, just as time is marked down and divided into neat, visible portions on the clock he bought for me: time to read, to think, to discuss the reading. For Patrick is a scientist, a man who believes in the reality of the world beyond our senses. And although I have reminded him that the past was once a part of that world, but is now taken within my memory and transformed, he sees the transformation as a sign that it is past, and no longer our concern. To think of it is my one remaining weakness; but that too can be transformed. The present is full of possibilities, while the past has none. I see him pointing at the clock as he says it.

Yet the dream I fell into, the clock was only brought to me. For it was while I was noticing that time had moved on to the slice between ten to eight and the hour, reminding myself that on the half hour he would be calling for me, that David came to my flat. When I heard the muffled knock I passed, as usual, from my bright sitting-room into the dark connecting hallway that gave access to the outside door. Only then, as I picked my way through the clutter of unopened boxes that had lain there since the move, was the knock repeated — his knock — and I stood still, recognizing it, although I know, because I have been told, that there can be nothing in that system of sounds which is peculiar to him. Nevertheless, I listened as the knock was repeated again without alteration; and when I touched the handle I felt the rhythm of its arrogance and the warm touch of sudden memory; at which I smiled, pulling the door wide open without further thought.

Bad, very bad, Patrick would have said, shaking his head at me. Very good too, as Stein might have added.

David was standing on the landing outside with one arm up against the doorframe and a bottle of wine grasped in his other hand. He was wearing a white cotton suit of 1980s design with a brilliant pink T-shirt beneath on which something was written. He smiled, and I noticed the unnatural whiteness of his teeth; just as I noticed that his hair was a darker brown than usual, than twenty years ago.

But I did not notice these things at that moment. I noticed them at leisure, in the long reflective space after the moment of action had passed. Within that moment, while I let him into the flat, found some glasses for his wine, I merely felt what I had felt so often when I was still living with him: both gathered and open, like a child hearing a fairy-tale, holding the ending like a slowly brightening bulb in its mind's eye; taking possession of it, glowing, radiating with that possession. Because that was what David had, a radiant personality that preserved him from blame, from any charge of abandonment, when he moved on between affairs as men in his profession invariably did; the women he left somehow shone into by him, roused into a certainty of being that did not fade but was permanently conferred, like a giving of grace.

But perhaps I forget. We were briefly engaged, but our engagement did not survive the constant fights. And when I say that it did not survive them, what is curious is that in the deep burst of truth which comes so often from argument we almost always revealed, not fundamental disagreement, but fundamental agreement; rather our wars were over dominance, the right to lead, to own the energy and ideas which flowed from our battling. Yet that was not how others saw it. Those on the outside saw only a need to make peace over us, to make peace into a division of us as it could not be made between us. Patrick was not one of them; but he might have been.

David stretched out on the sofa, and put his feet up.

"We've got the band together again, you know. We're touring again."

"Really? Just the same old stuff?"

He looked annoyed.

"No, new stuff too. But we have to do the old songs, my love, to get them to listen to the new ones. It softens them up. Don't you remember?"

As he said it he leaned forward, tilting his chin towards me in a way that I did indeed remember. Sometimes, when I had woken in the night, I had tried to dredge for that memory, to bring it into the darkness I felt to be spreading across my heart. Occasionally, after many hours, it would come; but briefly, too briefly to do me any good. Now he had brought it back to me, but it was not the same. There were lines around his eyes, surplus flesh around his cheeks and neck. I felt a terrible pain, as if I were losing a dream of him that I could not bear to lose, as if my life as it had become was unendurable without that fantasy. And then I saw that ageing was painful for him too, painful in a way that it would never be for Patrick. Perhaps it was the shock of that fresh insight that made me speak; or perhaps it was my anger with him for bringing down the past with so hard a hand upon my neck. I do not know.

"You were so beautiful."

He grimaced.

"And you were so much in love."

He turned away from me, and filled the glasses. Slowly, silently, we each drank to our loss.

"So. What have you told him about me?"

He had emptied his first glass and was filling it again. Mine he had filled to the brim, as though it had been a pint of beer; I looked but did not touch, imagining that he intended me to spill it.

"Almost all that there was to tell, I suppose. Whenever the conversation slackens there is always you – always more of you."

"Did you tell him that you were in love with me?"

"I doubt if I used that word."

"Ah."

It was my turn to be annoyed.

"It wouldn't have mattered, David. You were in the past."

"I see. And where am I now?"

There was a silence. David continued to drink, to look steadily at me. He was sitting directly beneath the clock, but too far beneath it to allow me to check the time without betraying it by my change of glance. The onus was on me to speak, to justify the shape of my new life, to articulate joy out of the peace that Patrick had brought to me. Yet the only words I could convincingly have used were those that belonged to my time with David, that had I used them would merely have convinced him that spiritually I remained joined to him as to a Siamese twin. So I remained silent. I waited instead for David to put me out of my misery, which he did by getting up and bringing my drink across to me, squatting down in front of me so that I could see into the light of his dark eyes, as though I was peering into a pool of my own past. I felt as if the world beyond me had blurred and softened; my own sensations sharpened and brightened. And the years did not roll back but rolled together, transforming present into past, past into present; crashing as they met, vanishing before my eyes in the instant of contact. I felt sudden and overwhelming lust

18

for him, lust that struck my body and doubled me where I sat. As he opened his arms and came closer, I could finally see what was written across his chest. No message, no philosophy, no maxim to clarify my new life. Just a publicity T-shirt bearing his own name, above a heart with an arrow threaded through it.

"Give me a kiss for old times' sake."

I tried to shake my head. As I did so the fumes from his breath seemed to circle around it, like a gulp of wine rolled around the mouth. He laughed and brought my untouched glass between our two faces, putting it to my lips. He had not spilled a single drop.

"For your birthday, my love, I take away your consciousness. I give you back romance."

The buzzer on the street door went at twenty-five minutes past eight exactly. I did not see the time, rather I knew it to be so, just as I knew when I heard Patrick's deeply measured tones speaking to someone downstairs that he had allocated those few minutes to establishing himself with the doorman who provided security for the building, who questioned callers as they arrived, politely ascertaining their relationship to those above. David lay back on the sofa, squeezing my hand whenever I thought he was dozing, waiting with obscene cheerfulness for the introduction that he had promised himself. And as I listened to the muffled conversation downstairs I wondered suddenly how he had got past the doorman, how he had made sure that the first sign of his presence was a sound that I knew to be his; knew it in spite of re-education, of explanation, of new life. It occurred to me that the man downstairs had all along been his shadow, when I was convinced it was the other way round; that Patrick trailed David with his words as theory trails inspiration, trying to write it like a flat Earth into the past.

But this is the present. And it is not a new life, Patrick, not even a second life, the creation of a new way of being from reason, for creation does not proceed from reason. I am transformed, but from within: from that mysterious relationship between the experienced present and the internalized past. Joy, spirit, love: these are words from the old life, with me in this room as David is with me, real because they make the silence sparkle. There is no peace dividend but the lust of love and battle held hidden like a jewel in the hands; tossed upward, to prove its eternal shine, into the dark.

Finding Simon

She knows he's here somewhere. She takes off her glasses and brings the photograph closer to her eyes, until the lines of heads and shoulders become individual boys and girls with faces that she can focus on, one at a time. At the front, a row of girls, seated. Behind them, another row of taller girls, standing, only visible down to their waists, their hands hidden, their school cardigans buttoned or unbuttoned depending on their attitudes to authority. And at the back, a line of boys, raised up on a wooden form bought out of the gym. The ones from the not-yet-cleared slums in grubby shirts and jumpers, the village boys mostly in school uniform. There are three fair boys who might be him. One with mousy hair in a dark V-neck pullover with his head tilted to one side, looking shy, askance, at the camera. One very straight and thin and upright, hair wavy and combed sideways, a scholarship boy if ever you saw one. One smaller, with a wide, smiling mouth, eyelids slanting downward to the outer corners, hair thick and blond and almost straight.

Every so often she pauses in the search to look at herself. She's in the front row, right at the end, the only one without her hands clasped in her lap. Her hair is short, shiny, good-girl style. She's smiling uncertainly, wondering what's going on behind her. Her left hand rests on her gingham skirt, on the chair, as if she expects somebody to take it in their own. Her particular friend is next to her. Her other friends, the ones she still has all these years later, are at the far end of the row.

And he's in the row of boys behind her. Somewhere.

Of course she knows what he looks like now. At least she does at the moment, if she concentrates, if she puts down the photo and shuts her eyes until she sees the hall full of guests for Ray Clark's 50th, all the old crowd sitting on grey plastic chairs around long tables with the disco lights strafing the dusty floor. She can see Sian, a big girl in a sparkly blouse, leaning across the table to hear what Mary's saying, she can feel the swish of Sian's red hair and schoolgirl hairstyle that she's never changed, just like she's never married, never had kids.

Pauline's the one who gets them all together every year or so, the one who rings everyone up, ferries them around in her car so they can all get drunk, remembers birthdays and anniversaries and faces from years ago that nobody else can place. She's been out for a fag but now she's back in her seat beside Sian, tucking imaginary wisps of hair behind her ears as she's done for forty years, wearing her quizzical look that shows the wrinkles in her forehead and on the sides of her cheeks, the ones her husband's always joking about. She leans forward and shouts something down the length of the table, but the disco's so loud it's just her mouth widening, then closing, and a certain lift of her plucked-out eyebrows.

A name, anyway. A name that as she hears it almost, but not quite, has a face to go with it. Or less a face, more a sound stored in her head, like one of those tunes you learned when you were five and never forgot. The tune starts to play but he doesn't give it time, he's crossed the dancefloor and he's weaving in and out through the plastic chairs toward her and all she can manage is a wide-eyed look of recognition, a lie that isn't quite a lie. He moves as though he's young, he's tall and slim in a black jacket and white open-necked shirt, his fair hair is slick and up-to-date. He gets hold of her hand and kisses her cheek and uses her old name easily, as if it's still hers, as if he isn't having to retrieve it from somewhere else.

She finds herself on her feet, answering to it, standing next to him. Her brain is still repeating his name, calling it across a chasm as if she's waiting for someone to throw a rope over from the other side. They're talking, exchanging careers, listing all the family births and deaths of the last forty years, finding they still live within five miles of one another, words that are meant to chain themselves into some sort of connection between them but come out like his name, as faintly familiar sounds with no meaning. But what she's seeing is a blue-eyed young man taking in her hairstyle and the black ruffle on her blouse, standing closer than he needs to, saying things she doesn't know the answer to.

"You look great, really great," he says. "Just amazing."

She flinches. Looks at him, realizes he means it. Her skin burns as though he's slapped her, dealt her a glancing blow she didn't expect, did nothing to deserve. She can feel the sleeve of his jacket, cool up against her arm, she notices how close he brings his face to hers when she talks, how he seems to be on the edge of kissing her whenever his mouth widens, in the second before each laugh. Nothing else. She can't talk to him, she can't remember him. Something else has taken over, feeling, reflex, a twitching of the fingers that would happen whether she was alive or dead. She has to take his word for the past. Later, she thinks he jumped out of the water at her like a shining fish. And the water's past, or present, or both, or neither. She knows there are words you must say in return for a compliment but with the live wire running up her flesh they won't come.

But something has to come, words to keep them both in the air, hold them clear of the ground.

She says, "You're not so bad yourself."

He stays with her through a sixties medley, leaning close into her, his sharp profile flashing on and off with the lights, facing the party but with his body aligned with hers. He doesn't ask her to dance but every time the pink light flashes across their table she knows he's with her. She can hear the Beatles and Stones and Searchers and the part of her that's out with Sian and Pauline wants to run onto the dancefloor and mime to the excitement, to dance the elation away without ever touching anybody. And the other part, that's not gone dead, with his black sleeve and the hard line of his belt slapping it back to life, tingling like flesh fighting back after the dentist's injection. She hears nothing that he says until he turns and kisses her again and shouts into her ear with his bottom lip up against the brass drop of her earring.

"I told Pauline I always fancied you. It's brilliant seeing you again."

She's yelling something in the well of her throat that neither of them can hear. Don't leave. Give me a bit more time and I'll remember, I'll know what to do. But her mouth moves as though it's repeating what he says, word for word, learning his words.

And he's gone.

She can feel Sian and Pauline looking at her, watching her back into her seat. Pauline raises the ridge of her eyebrows and checks her watch to see if it's time for another fag. Sian leans forward on her elbows and says in her deep mock-sexy voice

"And who was that good-looking young man?"

Simon, she says, Simon. We were at primary school together. Before your time.

Pauline's asking if she wants another drink and she nods. She's looking at her hands, she can't quite work out why. In the meantime the disco's moved on to the seventies and the Bee Gees and Sian just has to do her John Travolta party piece that always had them all in stitches so the two of them get up to dance. While Sian stamps her feet and punches the air she's circling in her own patch of floor space, arms hanging by her sides, spinning every so often on her axis but each time coming back to where she started, a yard or so from Sian's sparkly flailing sleeves. They dance without looking at one another, within invisible bubbles, on separate planets. And it's while she's coming off one of the spins she realizes that the blood doesn't reach her hands, that what she needs is something in her hand, a card with a number on it, an email address written on her palm, a sheet torn from her diary with only-just legible writing on it.

But she has none of these things.

She opens her eyes.

The photograph's still there on the table in front of her, dished slightly, the light from the window reflecting off its shiny surface. She picks it up and her eyes go straight to the boy standing third from the right-hand end of the row, the smaller boy with the smiling mouth. It's partly the downward-slanting eyelids but mainly the smile. There's no reason he shouldn't have grown taller in his teens, no reason why she can't be sure except she isn't. He smiles out at the camera, beyond the photograph, his left arm across his pale jumper, his dark tie slightly crooked, his hands hidden behind Pauline's dark head.

She thinks of writing to Pauline, who'll be sure. Forming words to disguise the not-words, replaying the party, asking for other names to lose his among them. She thinks of it until the party is a week ago, already becoming less than real, until the sharp lines start to go from Simon's profile, the energy from his voice. Finally there's a writing pad on the table with the photograph beside it and a pen in her right hand, a blank sheet of paper in front of her. Inside the photograph, the boy with the wide smile still looks at the camera while the girl with the short shiny hair does the best she can, sitting so far away, her head tilted as if she's listening for a whisper.

Hi, Pauline, she begins, and stops, looking down at her hands. But it isn't the pen-hand she's watching. It's the left hand, the one she doesn't use, still held out, waiting for somebody to take it.

REPOSSESSION

It's strange about what kills people, she said to him the first time they met. It's not the usual things at all, the long words on the certificates. Being overlooked is what kills, not mattering is what kills. Trying to be noticed and having all your edges planed away until you're just like other people, only less. And he was listening, really listening, or at least looking at her; because he was young too, then, and gorgeous, with eyes like old cognac; but he didn't stay, and the next man did, so the next man became her husband. The years went by after the husband killed her, yet she still walked and talked, so that perhaps she only had that condition Ray Milland had in the movie; and she made herself as still as her husband was, just the eyes staring out and waiting and remembering, and holding on so tight you'd never see unless you looked, really looked. And she stayed youthful and pretty and took to crystals and chanting and cognac, especially cognac; and there was a bit of Buddhism thrown in there somewhere, because she never killed: not spiders, not flies, not even those sad slow armoured beetles that patrol the floor; and she went out twice a week for lunch to lose herself in company, but Saturdays she spent alone.

And on a Saturday, which the husband always spent fishing at an artificial lake nearby, the first man came back. The husband knew when he let himself in with the trout stinking and swinging heavily from their hooks like clock-weights that she would be resting on the bed as she always did on a Saturday afternoon. He didn't call up, knowing she would be lying on her back with her arms straight beside her and her eyes staring upward and some foul-smelling oil burning at her side; and the bed neatly made, bedcovers pinned tightly down as they only did in hotels. He went into the kitchen and dropped the fish in the sink and washed his hands over them and they floated, silver and dead with open gasping mouths and emptied, unreproachful eyes, on the bubbling, fizzing water.

And then, when the husband went upstairs to change his clothes, he smelt a different smell: an old, familiar, embarrassing smell, a smell out of context; and instead of seeing her door closed with its Tree of Life poster and the painted tendrils on the door-frame in front of him he thought himself inside the room with the source of the smell, pinned paralyzed against the wall while the burglar or rapist did his worst.

But when he went in, there was no-one there.

He searched for her everywhere he could think of long before he reported her as missing. He was afraid of the questions at the police station, the description they would demand of him, the details about eyes and hair and idiosyncrasies he couldn't answer. He walked all around the village, visiting every shop and park bench, fetching up last at the pub where they went for their twice-weekly outing; but the only thing out of place was a middle-aged couple kissing in a corner; only really kissing, with stretched mouths and strange subterranean movements in their cheeks like eels twisting under sand; and two brandies and soda, both untouched, on the table before them. The husband looked around, looked at the drinks, and went home.

As she had still not returned by the following Saturday he went fishing as usual. The lake moved against his waders gently with a few dead-calm ripples, the sun shone, his float leaned on the water like the earth on its axis. After a couple of hours of catching nothing he lit a cigarette and looked upriver and saw a woman coming along the bank toward him. A youngish woman, long hair swinging side to side, long hair shining wet in the sun, white blouse sparkling like the water. She had reached the circumference of his umbrella and stopped before he recognized her, before he had time to think of how poorly she fitted the description he had finally given to the police. Just as he was opening his mouth to say a name he noticed the beating pulse in her cheeks and he had a sudden and absolute conviction that she was going to kill him; and he took a step backward, while she moved around the umbrella and bent and jerked the rod from its stand and dragged the line in, until the float wobbled and rolled in undignified extremity on the bank and the silver hook gleamed and trailed a length of green weed behind it. He tried to catch it and lost his balance and his footing in the mud, tumbling backwards onto the riverbank with the sun in his eyes and his waders writhing and glistening in mid-air, gasping for breath as she looked over him, gazed off into the distance.

He called out then. But not once did she look at him.

She was still for a minute. Then without a word she turned and retraced her steps along the bank and got into the car waiting upstream with its engine running. She put out her arms and gripped the dashboard tight until she remembered and let go and lay back with the movement and the strange new feeling of the double pulse in her hand, the strange echo of her name running after her. And as long as the man with the eyes like old cognac stayed with her, she never killed again.

Sleeping Beauty

He met the married couple in the village pub, not long after his divorce had come through, and the world he found himself in was still soft enough to take new impressions. They remembered his face from a series of classic roles he had played on TV during the seventies: Ariel, Chéri, Demetrius, but they remembered different things. The husband talked quotations and productions until his words yellowed and dropped like a stain on the objects around them; the wife kept her head down and her voice muted until, at last, she raised her head and looked at the actor and said: You wore a lilac shirt when you played Chéri. I remember all the colours, but the lilac best of all. You have to be very dark to wear lilac. The husband gave an embarrassed laugh and squeezed her hand, but the actor was flattered and revived in a breathless way that was strange to him, and he stayed with them for the rest of the evening, while Steven's monologue drifted like smoke around them. He watched the shifts in her gaze, her dull eyes fixed on the huddles around the bar and on the gleam of brass and brown tilted liquid; he watched her sudden bright eyes, when they fastened on the hair he kept longer than was fashionable, the hair he kept dark at heavier expense. By the time they had all given hands and names, he had her invitation in his hand and Steven's directions in his head; and he said, See you next Saturday, then, and turned his back and made his exit slowly, with the feel of her hands in his hair like a slow stroking ripple of applause.

And outside, in the dark night air, when he thought of their stillness as a couple; his by his own design, hers by someone else's, the vigour flowed in him as years ago, when he had taken on a new role.

What he could see of the house rising up on the billow of its surrounding wilderness looked fin de siécle; he thought he glimpsed the edges of crenellations and turrets, or perhaps only ornate and fantastically tiled chimneypots; the garden facing him through the spiked iron uprights of the gates destroyed all sense of scale. He spoke into the grille beside them that spat static back into his face and heard her whisper Hi, and said: It's Paul. We met — and one of the gates moved inward, surprisingly silent, before he had finished. Beyond the sweep the drive became grassy, shaded first by trees and then brambles, tough stems mounding on their layers of dead and fruiting wood and prospecting outward with virulent green suckers. As he contoured around them he caught metallic glints far back in the piled gloom. What looked like a watch hung from a twig, a thin chain twined two leaves together; closer to the drive scraps of fabric flickered in the branches, handkerchiefs or knotted flags with their colours fading. He found himself thinking of eastern religions, of souls fluttering in mountains where the air was stretched too thin; he thought he was in Poe, or Stoker, or du Maurier at least, but it was the first guess that clung to him as he bent to free his ankle from the branch that trailed and tugged at it and finally released him whiplike, with a lashing rebound.

Then he saw the scratches on the backs of his hands. And the Gothic door, with her standing outside it, wearing a long green dress.

"I'm sorry," she said in her faintest voice. "Most people bring their cars round the back."

"I'm banned," he said, "I got a lift. I'll wash it off, it doesn't matter."

"Of course it does," she said, frowning at the red on flesh-tone. "For you, it matters."

He saw Steven miming and beckoning from a window. She turned and touched his hand and the touch was not a hint, but a part of an action, yet to be completed.

"He's explaining to his friends how you came the wrong way. He'll make a joke of it, a kind of parable. He makes a joke of everything."

He followed her into the light and the pockets of noise and laughter and curious, incurious glances. Steven greeted him loudly and propelled him into groups with the dead weight of a hand upon his shoulder and introduced him as 'our classical actor friend. See if you can get him to tell you what he's doing now.' The men quickly lost interest in his account of provincial theatres and Shakespearian readings, while the women recognized him in a flash of excitement that passed mindlessly through their numbers like a Mexican wave. They moved in a circle around him, scanning his face for signs of corporeal decay, for the slow fall of flesh from cheeks exposed in profile, the bottle-sheen of the hair she had wanted to touch. He skimmed every encounter and held his hands up for excuse and then looked for her in corners and landings until he found her in a child's pose on the topmost stair with her arms around the carved rose finial of the banister. She dropped her head and smiled and he joined her.

"Your husband tried to revive the corpse of my old triumphs and his friends looked for new ones. They failed, so I've escaped."

"Good," she said, "Good. Now we have to see to your hands."

He looked at them. The streaks were dry. Her touching them would make them wet and stinging once again. Her touch would be soft, it would smell of old-fashioned balm. It would be a continuation of the action —

"Come and see my bathroom," she said.

The colour-scheme in the fragrant room was green and lilac. He washed his hands in lavender soap and looked at the bottles and compacts and tubes arranged on a shelf that ran almost round the room, displayed so that the word that appeared on every label faced outward. He scanned the shelf more than once, in case there was a rogue product without it; but she was consistent.

"This is my beauty circle," she said, dripping water very gently over the backs of his hands, "it keeps the ugliness outside at bay. But it's just a word, until it is embodied." She looked up at him. He could hardly hear her voice. "You embody the word. You're beautiful."

He followed her down the corridor like a drunk wrapped inside and out in fog; exhilarated, oblivious of harm.

She opened the door and the room stretched out before him, high and spacious, like a gallery. This room also smelt of lavender, unless he had brought the scent in with him. The only light was spot-light, each arc hung over a dark-framed print, and prints enough to cover every wall; typical Victorian subjects, richly coloured pictures of trysts in forests, abbey ruins, country chapel porches, women on pedestals and men on their knees. A woman sprang out of blossom to entwine a naked youth, a woman perched on a rock with a dark desperate man in the water beneath her; a young aristocrat lay cold, his dark head hanging backward, his white shirt open and his white chest catching the light from the half-open window. She was the guide, but with the siren's hair and distant gaze, circling her gallery with her hand trailing until he took it, and another part of the action fell into place.

She turned slowly, dropping his hand and finding it again, bringing her gaze back to him, letting it rest there.

"I looked for you here after we met last week but I didn't find you. You made the faces look different, somehow; I don't like them as much as I did."

He found the edge of a sofa nest-lined with shawls and pulled her gently down into it. Her body dropped graceful, slow-motion, against him, her eyes considered the circled naked youth opposite them on the wall. She read out the legend inked in Celtic script around the border.

"What I mean by a picture is a beautiful romantic dream of something that never was, and never will be." She twisted round and looked at him; and there was something sudden as he returned the look, a tremor in his view of her. "He should have said the world is ugly, and I hate it. I've said that, seen it many times. Only you came out of it, and now I'm not so sure."

"I'm sure," he said, putting his fragrant hands behind her head. "You want something real."

He kissed her and pulled her lips into a yawn and laid his cool tongue over hers and left it there for a minute so that they were like sleepers together. She slid slowly down the sofa with a lovebird shawl behind her head and the green dress slipping up her body and he saw with a second tremor that she was naked underneath. She parted softly, each flesh-layer sinking inward for him like a pressed rose, yet not too easily, so that the third tremor only came when it was over and she hugged him to her and rolled them both until she sat astride him and pulled the dress-folds from round her neck and flung them away from her, into the gloom.

"Again," she said.

He had a brief, faint echo of the sensation that sometimes came to him when he realized, all at once, that he was very drunk; then he looked at her, and saw the husband's stillness broken out of her; and smiled, and did as he was told.

"You must always wear it like this," she said, "just this length."

Her hands were in his hair, combing and pulling the thick fringe down over the lines on his forehead. Her damp fingers smoothed out the shape of his eyebrows, her fingernail traced a pencil-line beneath his eyes, flicked the lashes and wondered at their length; her free hand cupped his chin and pushed upward, tightening the flesh around his neck. Then she bent and kissed him three times: lips on lip, lips on lip, lips and tongue to make a drawn Cupid's bow of him.

And then he had the fourth tremor, right through his body.

"I have to go to the bathroom," he said. "I need to get a drink."

"Don't be long," she said, watching while he looked for his jeans. "Remember the ugliness out there."

The landing light hurt his eyes after the gloom and the door was locked and as he put his ear to the wood he heard the shuffling of movement inside. He breathed rapidly, stepped away and looked back toward her door. Then the bolt clicked and Steven emerged with a glass in his hand; stopped, and looked at him.

"Hello, Paul," he said. "Having a good time?"

He tried to get past, but Steven stood his ground.

"I hope you're good," he said. "She likes them pretty, but they aren't always good. There's a long word for her condition, too many syllables for me to remember. It's not a word she likes, but a washed-up actor with no ties just fits her bill. She can't go out much, so we bring the entertainment in."

He burst out laughing and shook his head and swayed against the door-frame. His nose and cheeks and his head under its stubble-cut were red from party wine, his blue eyes gleamed with the first expected pleasure of the evening; his top lip lifted, isolated from the other, sufficient for a sneer. Paul stood still and watched and heard her faint voice calling through the door at his back. Then he said only:

"She was right about the world."

The laugh rumbled from deep down, cutting through her voice.

"And you're a bit long in the tooth for Chéri. But she'll never notice in the dark."

He roared again as Paul pushed past him and into the bathroom and slammed the green door. The incantation of her beauty circle bounced its mantra off the mirror and he bent over the basin and retched until his head throbbed with the smell and only the scent on his hands, held up in front of his streaming face, gave him any relief.

41

"I thought you weren't coming back," she said.

He came into the room and went up to the window and opened it. The horizon of the bramble-patch curved dark against the summer sky, the objects hanging from the branches twinkling like stars. Nothing moved. He could hear the clarity of party goodbyes and the slam of car-doors and shot-bursts of laughter drifting from the other side of the world.

"I thought I wasn't. Then I thought of something."

She got up from the sofa and he saw how gracefully she cried.

"You see I waited for you. And I have been waiting for you, Paul. All my life."

He shut the window and stood against it, his veined hands laid gracefully on the sill.

"I'm taking you away," he said. "No evil husband, no galleries of men, no barbed horizon. Just you and me and happiness."

She twined her arms around him and he felt her hands, deep and deeper in his hair.

"In the morning," she said.

LAZARUS

I buried him myself. Deep, in the graveyard of the village where I used to live. It took me the whole of the longest night of the year, shovelling soil in the dark until there was no more soil, and when it was all gone I emptied my library of hard-backed books and piled them on top of him and added a few stones for good measure. It took all the books and stones I could carry to weigh him down, because he was so light, as light as bones with his wispy hair and windblown hands and voice that shredded all the words he threw away.

And at dawn I went away and shut the churchyard gate on his words and wondered if they would make the grass grow, and the grass grew so long and green that I had to come and clip it once a week from that day to this; and whenever I was there at dusk and the pink clouds piled up in the west I would remember him, remember how light he was whenever he lay across me; I would feel a pinprick of sensation in my hand and it would stay with me as I walked back down the gathering darkness of the lane.

He came back once or twice over the years and flitted off again, but he chooses this day of all days to talk to me, leaning over my shoulder to look at the anniversary flowers in their plastic on the path beside the grave, letting his wispy hair flop into my eyes, his windblown hands flapping against my shoulders, his voice shredding his words into pieces.

"Is there a pulse?" he says in my ear, and dashes off to the far end of the graveyard.

He has on that white shirt with the braille stripe. The cuffs hang down below his finger bones. As if he was an angel. And pointing like one at the flowers.

"Lunaria," he says. "Myosotis, then lunaria."

I stand up. He squats down behind a gravestone.

"I'm alive," his voice calls out. "You buried me alive."

He frightens me for a moment into goose-flesh. But I don't panic, I think about it, I shake my head. He never knew any Latin. He couldn't be alive.

He gets up and there are grass-stains on the white shirt.

"You see?" he says. "Grass and soil and worms in the soil. The worms kept me from starving. And a lot of books, musty and so heavy I couldn't get up. All those years of smoking. Couldn't get my breath."

I'm not going to humour him. I'm dragging the brown stems from the vase and they lie like the slime of dead worms on the path. All those years. Smoke and unwashed clothes and a bed stinking of dead flowers.

"Lunaria," he says in my ear. "Funny thing about death. Death is good when it's a lid that gets fastened down. Not so good when it's a door that swings and spins you round. Back from death's door, that's me. Question of semantics."

Now I'm sure. He wouldn't know the meaning of semantics, as I might have said to him once.

He laughs, the laugh that was always more than half a cough, that carried him away once too often. I'm clearing up the plastic and dead flowers when he head-butts me from behind and lays me out along the path. The vase rolls away and a tongue of water shoots out in front of my grounded chin and follows it. The water wicks into my skirt, into my knickers, makes me smell like twenty years of water in the vase.

His damp hair flaps on my neck.

"Get your attention," he says. "I didn't die. Read the papers. Read the gravestone."

The weight lifts off my back. He was always so light, lying across me.

"I finished all the worms off years ago," he says. "I'm hungry."

And I'm getting up and dripping. Dripping water down my thighs, brown veins of it down to my ankles. I turn round and he's mostly bones and slept-in shirt and trousers and no angel in the fingers pressing on my wrist.

"You see?" he says. "I knocked you down. How's that for a dead trick?"

I get my wrist back. It's pounding like you do when you're very sick and your body's trying to heal yourself.

"If you ignore me I'll go back out there," he says. "I'll disappear but I won't be dead. There must be something better than worms outside."

I know it's just that he's forgotten. He's forgotten that he died, he didn't go away. He went away so many times it feels the same to him. He used those words, going away, so often that in the end just the shreds of them were left to slap in my face. The words and the smoke-cloud that came with them, that lingered for days in the bedroom. That killed him.

"I'm fed up with this," he says, twisting to look at the churchyard gate, his white cuffs swinging like the bell-sleeves of a saint. "I'm getting out of here."

But he can't, he knows he can't. Not unless I let him.

Suddenly he's behind me again, breathing smoke into my neck.

"Myosotis," he says. "You've kept me here against my will. You can't stop me."

But I know what to do, I've done it so many times before when he was still alive, I can remember. I'm dropping down, away from his words. I'm pulling out the stems of the new flowers and the purple ones especially and I'm racing now, to get them into the vase, into fresh water, before he starts on me again. And I hear something, the creak of the churchyard gate, and I relax, he won't stay around with a stranger coming up the path, already the flapping of those sleeves and hair is lighter, hardly flicking me at all.

"You're dead," I say to the vase, forcing the stems into the shiny metal holes. "Lunaria."

And I work on at the grave, cutting buds and shaping greenery, trimming the words from the grass, while the pulse gets lighter, runs down into nothing, too faint to even be a pinprick when the pink clouds pile up in the west, when it's time to go back down the gathering darkness of the lane. The purple flowers have to be thrown away, they're drooping, nearly dead already. And I don't look round to see whether the gate's standing open because there isn't any point, I know how to tell when he's gone. Stink of dead flowers in the bed, how I always knew, waking in the morning and knowing he was so light I'd never felt him leave.

BLEAKLOW

It's not a mountain as such, she tells him, though it's high enough to qualify. More a name to walk into, a place in a sea of wild places. Seven miles from anywhere, a few sandy rocks in a sullen sea of peat. She has the map spread out to show him, flattening the creases so the space of whiteness with its faint brown contour lines looks emptier, running her finger along the route, over the blue veins of rivers with names like Spring Gutter and Miry Clough and Grinah Grain. The names carry her voice upward like a singer stretching for a high note. Mike looks and nods and agrees because he knows they're going anyway, whatever he says. He keeps his own counsel over whether she'll stay the course or run down like a dodgy battery after a few miles, burn out on all that fresh air, all those relentless sullen peat-clogged footsteps. But she's still talking in that bright voice she always had at the start of things, the one he remembers from way back, and the brightness gets into him. He makes the sandwiches, the flask of tea. Packs the haversacks, putting all the lighter things in hers.

She's leading as usual, humming a tune to herself. The path runs along the edge of Alportdale like a visible contour line across the moor. The valley with its dark patches of conifer plantation drops away at her left side, narrows and loses definition the further north they go. They've had morning tea beside a few indifferent sheep, they're at 1600 feet and going strong.

So far they've seen no one else. After the halt the thin dark lines of other people appear, further back along the path. Two couples, perhaps half an hour behind them. And much closer, a young man on his own except for his two dogs, striding out, gaining on them. At the first opportunity she walks off the path and pretends to be looking at a bird across the valley so he can pass them, nodding a greeting over her shoulder as he draws level. When the back of his blue cagoule and red rucksack is turned towards her she watches him. The dogs are nice dogs, Border collies. One collie is on the lead, the other roams but not quite freely, running off the track then looping back to its master. The collie on the lead is the troublesome one, the potential sheep-worrier, keeps on looking back. The man is tall and lean with fair hair. He's a strong walker, doesn't stop, could keep on going for ever. He has a look of Philip in his steady head and easy stride, Philip in his fell-running days. She doesn't know whether they've both noticed it.

It's moorland weather. The sky is high grey cloud, a flatness over everything, that could melt away by lunchtime or drop down without warning on their heads. She wonders if Mike's packed the compass but she doesn't ask, not yet. They've stopped so he can fix the slipping strap on her rucksack and the lone walker has pulled away another half mile in front. The path is no longer smooth, it falls apart into pale sandy rubble, it disappears abruptly into peat-groughs, steep miniature valleys with sides of dark brown compost that can suck their boots away if they jump down. They go round for firmer ground, arcing and splashing through red marsh-grass, spooking the grouse and the white mountain hares. She's glad to see the wildlife. The back part of her brain wants something there especially for Mike, some balance for her neediness. The more so because he'll never ask.

There are no real hills here, just swellings in the ground. The solitary walker disappears in each dip then reappears, a vertical speck and two horizontal ones, one close, one circling. He slants across the sweep of heather on the next rise and she exclaims, she can't see the path at all, just him. That's enough though. If truth be told, she doesn't really read the map. She plans and daydreams with it but hardly ever uses it outside. Her routefinding is a kind of sleepwalk in which she retraces tracks. Footprints left by strangers or people she's forgotten but most often Philip's tracks, always ahead of her, leaving muddy prints for her to follow. Deep studded marks in the peat like those left by his running shoes, the ones she kept in the belowstairs cupboard for a year after he'd gone.

Today they have two sets of pawprints criss-crossing them.

Bleaklow comes steadily closer. First it was hardly there at all, a long grey mass in the distance, stretching itself across more and more of the view. Now it's a solid level ridge with a clear outline and outcrops of large pale boulders lighting up the horizon. Mike says he can see the strong walker on the final slope, meandering with the path, heading for the largest outcrop, but she can't get a fix on him with her binoculars. They're near the top now, in a moonscape of groughs where they walk on the exposed stone at the bottom with walls of black peat around them, too high to see over. She enjoys the strangeness of it, the winding, the firm sandy floor with the trail of prints and hoofmarks. They'll catch the lone walker on the top, leaning against a boulder with his back to them and a corned beef sandwich in his hand. The loose dog lying down, head on paws, sweeping the white sand with its tail. The other dog whining, circling, watching its master. Watching everyone who comes and goes.

Suddenly they're up. The land flattens out and new land appears. The long thin mast of Holme Moss transmitter drops a plumbline into a world of horizontals, the moors close up and lose the valleys between them. There are people and rucksacks tucked into gaps between the white stones that provide the only shelter from the wind, but the solitary walker is missing. She wanders around the outcrops saying she's looking for the Anvil Stone to photograph, finds it, checks her watch. Mike suggests a rest for lunch. No, she says, across at Grinah Stones, another mile or so, before they start on the descent. Her voice is duller, tired for the first time since they started. The groughs in the depression are deeper and more unrelenting, they're not a moonscape any more. She jumps down into soft peat walls and scrambles out of them, boots clogged and heavy, groaning each time she clambers up. They're chilled and exhausted by the time they arrive at Grinah Stones. The grey sky finally takes a decision, starts to sink down on their heads.

"It knows how I feel," she says, crouching by a sandy rock, trying to get her glove off, pulling the map from a pocket in her fleece.

Mike's heard this kind of thing before and there's nothing you can say. It's her religion, tougher than the usual kind, its miracles and terrors made of soil and stone and sky. She can point at these things and prove their power to him. He's given her the compass and she's turning her open palm this way and that, while the red and white pointer shudders in its case and waits for her hand to settle on a direction. The sky drops further, greying out everything except the crop of boulders they're sitting on and the dark hump of heather next to them.

She starts to cry.

"I'm lost," she says. "I've never been here before. I don't know where I'm going."

He's used to the pronoun, so used to it he's almost come to think it really does include him. She has the map in her other hand but she's not using it. She's holding it out in front of her with the misty land beyond, as if she sees no connection between them at all. There's a blind look about her eyes, the look she had that day when she passed the phone to him without a word, the look she still wears first thing in the mornings when she remembers. His heart sinks. Down below he sees a few isolated fence-panels stuck into the spongy ground, most probably rough shooting-butts. He points to them and then to the map, but he won't try to take it from her, he knows better than that. She won't listen to him, she'll never follow him. The one who goes first, goes first.

It starts to rain. Mike unpacks his bag to get at the cagoules but she's rooting round inside her haversack for a Tupperware of food. She's stuffing bread into her mouth and shivering. Getting the haversack back on, strapping her trekking pole around her wrist.

"Down," she says. "You don't care if I freeze here. I'm going down."

For a moment he can't see what's set her off. Then he spots the dark line of a figure on the blur of moor below, traversing right to left across their view. A walker on his own. Not a dog in sight. Without another word she's started off straight down between the boulders, lurching side to side through stones and mounds of heather, stumbling and yelping so it'll be a miracle if she gets down without a broken ankle. He tells her to slow down, but it's more for him than her. The recklessness is Philip all over, Philip on a scree-run in the Lakes with the pebbles raining down and the whole hillside turned into a waterfall while the mortals down below gawped upward in amazement. She loved to watch from high up on the crag but she didn't have the nerve to follow, his confidence that taking risks was the safest thing he did. She knows this as she knows he's gone, he isn't coming back. But she won't stop, she'll refuse to use the words. There will be other words instead, words Mike can translate but never answer. He shoulders his haversack and goes after her.

Where the slope eases she can see no tracks. Her mind is full of mist, mist crackling like the static on a radio. Being lost is to have no signs, no marks left in the ground. She's disappearing, like the Invisible Man, her fleece zipped up over her lack of substance, less real than Philip's footprints. Nothing is real unless you see it. Bleaklow too has withdrawn into the mist, retreated back inside its name. The heather turns to pale tussock grass scored by a wide depression, a kind of dike running lengthways away from her. Even the walker has disappeared. Perhaps just over the next rise in the ground, but it doesn't matter any more. She resumes her stumbling run, following the dike wherever it goes. She's forgotten maps, forgotten what they're for.

As they lose height the mist begins to thin. Two more walkers appear, some way ahead, also following the dike. A couple, both with dark cagoules and trekking poles, a man and a woman with grey hair, ambling and talking as they walk. They can't see her yet, she's still invisible. But she's gaining on them, within shouting distance, speaking distance. Behind her Mike trots through boggy grass with the rucksack bouncing and thumping on his back, watching as her shape converges with theirs, although they're lined up so perfectly in his sights he can't really see how close she is. The thought dawns on him that she's going to ask the way. He stops and waits, heart pounding, out of breath. He knows that if this happens, then everything will change. Not only Bleaklow. Everything.

And then she stops too, as if the message passed straight from his mind to hers. The couple keep on walking. Soon their shapes are separate from hers again, different sizes.

She turns round and waits for him. Points forward.

"There," she says. "See the towers? Howden Reservoir. Shireowlers Wood. Abbey Clough."

These names sound different to the ones she read to him off the map. She draws them round her in a way you couldn't do with Bleaklow. Her voice is used to them, dips half an octave with relief. The treeline looms up just ahead, a dark block of spruce where they'll be lost to sight. They drop down onto a forestry track leading through the woods and the moors are gone. Mike rubs his eyes, glad to be done with distances and horizons. He's leading now, not looking back. He hears the scrape of her trekking pole as she drags it behind her, her voice complaining that her knee has gone. The thud of her feet in her conscious limp. He looks at his own feet, heading downwards to the gate at the end of the track. The descent is soothing. He slows down, prolonging it.

Through the thinning trees a bike with a Lycra-clad rider flashes past. The road is just below them. Then the bridge that carries it across a moorland stream, then the long flat grey of the reservoir. Mike finds a spot for them to rest beside the stream and wait for the bus back to the car park. Some Canada geese come up to share their belated lunch but she shoos them away and tries to coax a chaffinch with some crumbs. The cold is a gift sent after them from Bleaklow, a distant sun wrapped tight in mist. They drink their second cup of lukewarm tea in silence. Other walkers stomp down from the heights to catch the bus, calling out enquiries to each other about the day, shouting jokes across the stream. He watches them over the bridge, knows the exact moment when they get too close.

"Shall we move?" he says.

But she isn't looking. She's staring across the reservoir to the level track above its eastern shore. She lifts her binoculars to her eyes. Points.

"There he is," she says. "On the other side, with two dogs. It's him, isn't it?"

Looking with the naked eye Mike can just see a moving figure with two long dark specks some way in front. Probably a dog-walker doing the circuit of the lake, it's round about the time. He shakes his head but she doesn't see, she's turned towards the growl of engine-noise sounding through the trees.

The bus is coming. She gets up, brushing crumbs from her fleece, her voice suddenly turned upward again, bright with the start of things.

"You know what?" she says. "I want to come back and do this walk again. Get it right."

Mike empties the rest of the tea into the grass to lighten the bag. Then he bundles everything inside his haversack, shoulders it and follows her, heading for the bus.

THE GARDEN

Monday morning. Down the road at number 40 the landscape company's truck is unloading men and tools ready to finish preparing the front garden for block paving. All weekend the JCB has lain still and silent, squatting in the small square plot like an orange cuckoo. On Friday its engine hummed all day, had the garden scooped up by teabreak at three o'clock. Eileen watched the corpse go off in the skip from an upstairs window. There were thick chunks of turf and ragged dry clumps of hedge, privet roots sticking out from the top of the pile like old skinny legs. And two mallow bushes that were planted in the centre of the lawn. Grubbed up a few weeks before flowering time.

The woman at number 40 looks pleased. She's standing hands on hips talking to the IT specialist who lives further down the road, the leafy part with the big detached houses. He doesn't bother with her normally, apart from a brief Good Morning wave, but the excavation inspires respect, gives them a common frame of reference. There are cars and children to be accommodated and not enough time in the day for lawns, so the paving will be more practical all round. What can you do with a front garden in this day and age anyway?

What can you do?

Eileen takes her tea into the back garden, leaving the door swinging on a piece of string, because otherwise the wind will blow it open and smash it loudly against the side of the house. She wanders across her weedy crazy paved patio, down the three slate steps and onto the lawn. Blades of long grass spill into the pond like an overgrown fringe, the plump seedheads blow clouds of pollen out above them. Fescue, bents, the quaking grass with its thin quavering stems, that she planted years ago in the border and found its own way here. Under the grasses in the greenish water male newts jockey for position and flick tails while the females lay their eggs calmly on the crowfoot fronds, sticking their babies' feet out at right angles to their peanut-shaped bodies. Eileen doesn't know how many newts there are but she thinks they ate the tadpoles up this year; something must have done, because the frogs spawned like they always do and the spawn sank to the bottom of the pond and lay there, billows of it, like heavy clouds under a thick green sky.

But there were no tadpoles. Next year she'll have to fish out some spawn and keep it in a bucket with some weed for a few weeks until the tadpoles grow legs, until they're big enough to cope with the newts. Maybe she shouldn't interfere but she always does, after all even a nestbox counts as interference and she has three, although so far this season only one's been used. Eileen didn't see her blue tits fly the nest but she thinks there were four or five of them. When the adults stopped feeding she got the wooden stepladder out from the back of the shed, cleaned the spiders' webs off it and put it up against the big birch, climbed unsteadily up and opened the lid of the box. There were two little dead ones, tiny scraps of claw and dark blue skin wrapped in moss and wispy feathers. She took them out very carefully and buried them in the loamy soil under the hawthorn hedge at the bottom of the garden, still wrapped in their soft dry moss. Poor little birds, she said as she buried them. Since then she's said it to herself, several times a day.

Poor little birds.

The steps seem to have got heavier. She had to stop twice dragging them back to the shed, pushing them into their space beside the lawnmower. Aluminium ones would be more practical but Joe did all his painting from these, splashing about with powder blue and cherry red and Laxton's Green until each tread looks like a Jackson Pollock canvas. There are colours on here long since painted over in the house, pictures of rooms and times that she's forgotten. One thing she did notice, putting the steps back, is that the strut fixing them in place is split and she doesn't know how to mend it.

She also noticed how long the back hedge had grown, how the rose and bramble suckers looped and whipped around in the wind way above her head. She'll try and cut it later on.

A hard, rhythmic thumping sound is coming from down the road. It thunders through the ground, like an earthquake, or the bass beat from the music at a party. It cracks the soil with a low-frequency vibration, deep down, rattling the roots of the plants like sudden mining subsidence, opening up fissures that run from one garden to another. The landscapers are flattening the earth with the backs of spades, or one of those pneumatic punches that road-builders use, pounding the ground into submission. Far below the surface worms burst open, snails crumble into silver dust, beetles crack. The soil is squeezed into granite, compressed so that the rain will never penetrate it again but lie in dull pools on the surface till it's burnt off by the sun. In a couple of days the clingfilmed cubes of paving will be unwrapped and the garden will be gone forever, sealed like an Egyptian pyramid or a stone sarcophagus ready for the wheels to roll across. From the bedroom window Eileen can see the cars waiting in line, silver roofs shining in the sunlight. She goes back down into the kitchen, puts the kettle on, listens as it boils, listens as it cools down.

Finally there's silence.

A groove has appeared in the grass, like the trail of a cat or a fox, where Eileen has dragged the steps down the length of the garden. The groove winds past the pond down the rough path through the vegetable patch and under the straggly apple trees to the back hedge. Joe used to say a once a year cut was all it needed; he'd take the steps round to the lane at the back of the houses and clack away with the shears until she saw his white sunhat appear above the beech and flowering holly and the privet from the kitchen window. Since the land at the back was sold you can't get into the lane anymore, so Eileen will just have to do her best from the inside. She plants the steps as firmly as she can, pushing them into the base of the hedge, and climbs up onto the second tread. This is her favourite, the one with the splash of sunrise yellow dribbled with grey and large blotches of a kind of brickdust pink that didn't go with anything so they painted it over with something that used to be called sage green, which actually looked more like the colour of rosemary. From her slightly elevated position the garden glimmers at her, a light clearing between swags of cherry and oak, branches dipping heavily in front of her. Four young wrens are churring at the top of the tallest birch, gorging on greenfly and brilliant blue flies that drop onto Eileen's hair like a beaded hairnet. She peers into the hedge, looking for the nest. A wren's nest is a secretive thing, a tight ball of leaves and moss often buried in a dark fork of beech. The female will fly discreetly, keeping under cover of the trees and branches, when visiting it. Mostly the first you know of nesting wrens is a group of young ones flitting round after their parents, or huddled together deep in the shrubbery, a mass of brown barred feathers and soft thin beaks.

She can't see the nest. As she leans further in the steps start to tip, and she gets down and moves them into a steadier position before climbing up again.

This time she'll need to climb to the top to start cutting. The fifth step is, as it were, the platform; less blotches here, but overlapping circles of different colours like a dismembered rainbow, showing where Joe put down the tins of paint. Even standing up here isn't really high enough; the dog-rose sucker still curves well above her head. Eileen gets a hand on it to pull it down towards her. The long tough stem is trimmed with pale leaf-bracts and very small pink roses with a single layer of petals and the yellow thready centre exposed, the way all roses used to be.

There's a sound of screeching far above her. She looks up, leaning back against the birch to get a better view. Very faint in the sky, the dark arrowheads of two swifts, feeding, wheeling around. Swifts are almost mythical birds, only ever seen on the wing, only coming to earth when they're at the nest. She's always glad to see them, hear them, brave little birds dodging bullets and nets in Spain and Malta, gliding across African deserts, finding their way unerringly back to this precise piece of sky, this gap in her trees.

Always two of them.

The landscapers have packed their tools into the truck and gone. Just the lad left behind to finish up, hosing down the paving, concentrating the water-jet on every last bit of grit, any hint of grass or lichen in the gaps. A thin flood of silt runs down the drive, leaves a sandy tidemark on the road, trickles sluggishly down the drain. The lad finishes his fag, drops the end into the rill of water. He turns the outside tap off, gets his dusty denim jacket from the lid of the wheelie bin, goes off down the road texting on his mobile phone. The hose lies coiled on the stones, a drip of water forming every so often at its lip.

Mrs Watson, of number 40, sits in her front room, a cup of tea before her, looking out of the window. Sunlight streams in. A car races by, taking the rat-run short cut through to the main road.

Then nothing.

RESERVOIR

He's got the young collie with him in the van this morning. Excitable, like young dogs are, jumping over the back of the passenger seat and barking at anything that moves. He's old enough to know where they're going though. He barks when they get to the pull-in at the end of the track, when thcy park in front of the sign that says Anglers Only. Michael likes the sign, just as he likes knowing that his permit is zipped tight into the inside pocket of his jacket. He's never been asked to show it, but it's there.

He unpacks his gear, shoulders the wooden box by its long canvas strap, takes the rods in his other hand. Ben runs down the bank, off to the water's edge to get a sniff of the geese but he won't go far. Michael follows him, jumps down off the grass ledge onto the rocky shoreline. June, so the level's low. The high water mark is a brown line of twigs and pinecones and other rubbish. They settle themselves down a couple of feet below it and Michael starts setting up the rods.

Ben barks. The first car going along the road on the far side of the reservoir, sun flashing off its windows. They watch it speed past, heading for the best parking space at the Visitor Centre. The noise of the revving engine echoes across the space of the water. Later there will be more trippers, doing their Sunday circuit of the reservoir with their dogs and bikes and pushchairs. Not here, though. Anglers Only.

The car disappears behind a plantation of spruce and Ben lies down again, head on paws. Michael stops what he's doing to give him a pat. He's a young dog. No long-term memory. Like all dogs maybe. There's no way to know.

"There", she says, pointing at the far end of the lake just below the viaduct with the cars streaming across it.

He gets hold of the side of the leaflet that's flapping in the wind. His trekking pole clatters onto the stony track with a metallic sound. He leaves it there while she reads.

"It says this part of the valley was flooded in 1954. The village was demolished except for a few houses on the hillside. There was a final service in the church the day they left."

He looks at the smooth flat expanse of grey water in front of him. The pale shoreline on the farther side, dotted with a black beached boat and a couple of fishermen.

"Sad", he says.

She gets hold of the leaflet with both hands again.

"There's a story that the church bell still rings."

He laughs.

"There would be. Come on, before somebody else gets to that seat."

In a corner of the leaflet is a black and white photograph of a group of villagers standing in front of the church door. The men are bare-headed, their hats removed and held at their sides. You can't see the spire, but the leaflet says there was one.

"Why shouldn't it ring?"

"Because it's just one of those stories people tell themselves."

Michael walks into the water until it laps just above the knee of his waders. It's a strange sensation. Like being in another dimension, looking down instead of up, all the life under your feet. He's only a couple of yards out but already the stones of the beach are giving way to soft gravelly silt. He'll start to sink if he stands still too long. Sometimes he thinks that if he walked far enough he'd feel grass under his feet, grass still growing on the flooded fields. And, at the deepest point, the rush of the river flowing in its old bed, pushing against the resistance of his legs. Moving water. Living water. Different to the peaty smoothness of the lake.

He can feel himself sinking gently into the silt and takes a step backwards. Never let your mind go where your feet can't follow, his Dad used to say. Brown silt clouds the water and obscures the stones. Small stones, just the right size for chucking.

"Where's our house now, Dad?"

He's paddling, the gritty pebbles sharp on the soft soles of his feet. He turns and looks behind him. His father's squatting down, choosing a stone, his face shaded by the peak of his cap. Funny how that cap never falls off no matter how much he bends his head. Then he gets up and chucks the stone far into the lake. There's a solid, solemn plop. A pale ripple that doesn't reach the shore. Michael waits, turns and looks back again. His father's pointing, out over the reservoir.

"Go and fetch it then."

Dad laughs. It's a dry laugh, with all the energy drained out of it. Michael never forgets that sound.

Slowly he backs off, step by step, toward the beach. The silt sucks at his waders. A brown cloudy trail follows him back to dry land and

Ben, who's sniffing round the waterline. The dog wags his tail, looks expectantly at him.

The gravel crunches under his tread. Brittle, as if it was glass breaking. Don't let your mind go where your feet can't follow.

Nobody else has taken the seat, so they sit and eat biscuits and drink tea from their flask until it's time to leave the tarmac for the old road. The brass plaque on the seat reads: In Memory of Frank and Doreen Page of Macclesfield, who loved this place.

"I wonder if they knew the valley," she says, "Before as well as after."

"Unlikely," he says. "Not if it was drowned fifty years ago."

They walk on for a couple of miles in silence. Dust blows from the stony track and mists their legs. Although everything close to them is quiet, the drone of traffic from the viaduct ahead is beginning to be audible. The line of sycamores fringing the lane shades out the sun, conceals the few houses dotted around the hillside rising behind them. Where the shade is deepest the lane dips down towards reservoir level, curves gently around a bay and then emerges from the trees, pale and ramrod-straight.

Beside the lane in the dip there's a patch of waste ground covered in nettles. Mossy stones protrude here and there from the green stems. They might be old gateposts or the parts of walls or buildings sunk into the ground. She stops to look. It's dark under the trees, and the nettles are at least knee-high.

"It's a graveyard," she says.

He stoops to see under the unlopped branches.

"Could be. Hard to tell with all those nettles."

The leaflet comes out again.

"It doesn't show where the graveyard was. And it doesn't say what happened to the graves. There must have been graves, they must have dug the bodies up and buried them somewhere else."

While she's been talking he's gone on a few yards ahead, back into the sun, looking through binoculars at the car park on the opposite side of the lake. The cars flash on and off in the sunshine, as people arrive and leave and open and close doors. Like Morse Code. Alarming and perfectly logical.

"It's nearly full. Good job we were here early."

She comes after him.

"They must have done. Mustn't they? Buried them somewhere else."

He lowers the binoculars. The cars fade into the background, but the flashes remain.

"I suppose so, yes."

"But where?"

Ben barks. He's barking because Michael has caught a fish. The fish is a large blue carp with a gaping mouth, gasping in Michael's hand. Michael is holding the fish out away from him, as if undecided whether to kill it. Although he has never killed a fish, he can't bear that strange alien palpitation, the way the fish inflates and flattens in his hand as it gasps, he has to let it go. He removes the hook with shaking fingers and gently lowers the fish back into the water. He rarely has to do this. If it happened too often he might stop coming altogether. But his mother said you shouldn't walk away, you mustn't take your eye off what's important because that's when you lose it.

The fish gulps the water as if it was drinking and leaves Michael's hands. It's a blue curve in the brown water and then nothing. He takes his hands from the water and it's glass again, clear briefly to the pale pebbles on the bottom. She must have taken her eye off the church, but he never spotted it if she did. He can just remember her pulling him along the lane with the late Sunday bell ringing monotonously, dong, dong, dong, squeezing his hand with her white glove.

And it's warm through the glove, warm as it never is afterwards.

After she dies the gloves disappear somewhere. He finds coats and dresses and the butterfly scarf she always wore against the wind, but not the gloves.

He unhooks the rod from its stand and makes for the beach and his wooden box. He'll take his lunch hour but Ben will get most of the sandwiches. The dog is standing in the shallows, wagging his tail, giving short sharp single barks. Across the reservoir the picnics are in full swing, smoke rising from barbecues, kids shrieking and running in and out of the water like they're at the seaside. All water's the same to them. Just water.

She's clambered over the fence beside the lane and gone down to stand alone on the beach, to get closer to the water. The lake is blue and smooth, hardly lapping on the stones. Its great still body lies between her and the noise of people and traffic on the other side. There are pale sandy stones beneath her feet and she thinks of throwing one into the water but it would be the wrong kind of sound, the kind that's drowning out what she wants to hear.

All the wrong things have sounds, all the wrong things are silent. If the noise would stop for a minute she's sure she'd hear an echo of 1954, the scrape of people shutting their gates for the last time, the straining on canvas ropes of coffins dragged out of the ground, of all the silences that should have a sound. Though she wouldn't say so to him, she knows all feelings have echoes, she can't believe an echo ever dies away.

But the noise doesn't stop.

A dog barks, somewhere close to. She turns and looks along the shoreline. It's a black and white collie, standing on the beach about a hundred yards away. Close to the dog there's a man fishing, or rather packing up his fishing gear into what looks like a tea-chest. He hangs over the chest like a heron. He doesn't look up from what he's doing.

The dog doesn't bark again. They're nice dogs, those collies. It's wagging its tail already.

She clambers back up to the lane.

"Hear anything?" he says.

She takes her trekking pole from his hand.

"Only a dog. And there was a man fishing further on. I don't think he'd caught anything."

The lane ends about half a mile further on, at a five-barred gate with a tumbledown wall on either side. On the right of the gate the wall trails down over the grassy bank onto the lakeshore, loses itself in a scattering of stones sinking down into the water. Beyond the gate there's a patch of tarmac and then they'll join the road carried over the viaduct. The sound and brilliance of the cars is like a bright hard waterfall engulfing them.

He goes ahead, to open the gate. She walks through and then stops, waiting for him to close it.

VICTORIA

In 1968 the Victoria Railway Station in Nottingham was demolished to make way for a shopping centre. All that remains of the station in the 21st century, apart from the clock tower, is a deep excavation where the lowest level platforms were. In the 1990s a multi-storey car park was built inside this well-known 'hole in the ground'.

He says there used to be trains here. He says that if you stand and lean over the concrete wall at the north end of the car park you can smell the smoke coming out of that blocked-up tunnel with the little door in it. It doesn't matter what floor you're on. Doesn't matter that it's just a hole in the ground with a car park in it and grass and rubbish at the bottom and those purple plants growing all round the sides. Buddleias, he calls them. I lean over and count the white lines of concrete going down until I'm giddy and my thoughts kind of tipping out of my head and I can't smell anything. He says I'm not connecting. He says if you can connect the past with the present you'll be okay, you won't go mad. Odd for somebody who could drink White Lightning for England and been in and out of Saxondale so often, I say, but he says that was after, and he knows what was before. He connects.

The way he likes to tell it, he came into the world on an express train from Sheffield in a carriage without a corridor, sitting all alone with his drama diploma on his knee in a compartment with the red plush seat stretched edge to edge across the train, with the windows shut and the smoke piling up outside like grey cotton-wool in his ears. Then bursting out of the tunnel. The sun flashing semaphore round the clock tower and peaked caps on the station platform and his luggage on wheels with the weight taken out of it, rolling him up on the lift bearings right to the top of the hotel. Fancying he can just make out the prow of the theatre and the top curves of his Christian name on the poster through the gap in the frosted bathroom sash. And after the first night, chatting up his pick of the Osborne groupies on the strength of a treble Pimms with the fruit salad sliced like only they can in the County cocktail bar. Dropping off to sleep with the early morning goods to Loughborough pummelling his limbs with a good slow solid pulse.

But he's talking up the end of the old days from the footlights every night. Even Osborne'll go eventually, the goods, the smoke, everything but the hole in the ground and the clock and the hotel. Maybe they keep them so they can say they're connecting, maybe they lost their nerve in that clean concrete future at the last minute. You can shrug your shoulders and drive away or you can listen to his stories and wait for the past to get present again. And he's so well-connected, as I like to tell him, he just can't leave it alone. If some pissed punter gives us a tenner he'll say, Let's go to the Vic, and though they don't call it that any more the porter lets us in if we're not too scruffy, and we have proper drinks in a glass and talk about before. Or he does, and I just listen and think how I could have fancied him even more when his eyes were glossy and his hair not so worn out and he sat pointing forward, like he is in his old studio photos. After he's had a couple of Strongbows he gets up and walks round and shows me where he used to sit when it was a proper lounge with plush seats for all the actors to pose in and wait to be recognized. He tries it out in one of those hard-backed chairs and he sways from side to side, like he's in a fast train, like he's looking for arms that aren't there, and the porter comes to chuck us out. Sometimes he gets mardy and runs the back catalogue of the J B Priestley's and Agatha Christie's he played at the Royal but he generally looks at me and calms down and goes quiet enough. Only just this once he doesn't move, he's rewound to the beginning of Look Back in Anger, and he turns round so Jimmy Porter that for a minute the guy's stopped in his tracks. But he can't keep it up. I see it twitch on his face and it's gone. The guy asks us to leave again and makes to get on his mobile and we're walking out of there. And when I look at him, I know something's changed in the minute he eyeballed that kid with the regulation braided cuffs who's never lifted anyone's suitcase in his life. Something changed.

Anyway. This is where he fell, about six foot from that white pillar with Man U sprayed across it. First floor. Not quite the top, but far enough up to make it a decent drop. And he would never have done it, if they hadn't left this hole in the ground, if they hadn't given him the chance to connect. Because he didn't do it straight away, he waited till he smelt the smoke, till he saw the engine squeezing like black toothpaste from the tunnel, pushing up clouds as it braked. He reckoned he'd catch it while it was still moving, he thought it would be quick and it wasn't. And I couldn't lean over and see his face, I was looking round for something to hug and there was just cold concrete and nothing moving but those purple plants, clinging onto the side of the hole and waving with butterflies, dozens of them, flying all round them.

And I don't fancy working this place any more. I know it's a good pitch with people getting out their money for the car park but, as I said to the crowd down the Dog and Partridge, there's too much of him, too many connections for me. In any case he's snuggled up to me, cold hands in my pocket, whenever I smell smoke. Not 20 Dorchesters kind of smoke, but heavier stuff, what I like to call Victoria smoke. Our smoke. We're breathing it all the time.